THE
WINNER'S
WALK

THE WINNER'S WALK

Nancy Ruth Patterson

Pictures by
Thomas F. Yezerski

SCHOLASTIC INC.
New York Toronto London Auckland Sydney
Mexico City New Delhi Hong Kong Buenos Aires

ISBN-13: 978-0-545-10233-9
ISBN-10: 0-545-10233-2

Text copyright © 2006 by Nancy Ruth Patterson.
Illustrations copyright © 2006 by Thomas F. Yezerski.
All rights reserved. Published by Scholastic Inc., 557 Broadway, New York, NY 10012,
by arrangement with Farrar, Straus and Giroux, Inc. SCHOLASTIC and associated
logos are trademarks and/or registered trademarks of Scholastic Inc.

12 11 10 9 8 7 6 5 4   10 11 12 13/0

Printed in the U.S.A.   40

First Scholastic printing, September 2008

Lexile is a registered trademark of MetaMetrics, Inc.

For Ginger and Simon,
who taught me to love horses,
and for Pooh, Macon, and Newby,
who taught me to love dogs.
And especially for my father, Jack H. Patterson,
and for my grandfather, Norman H. McCune.
They, too, loved
"all things bright and beautiful,
all creatures great and small."

Acknowledgments

Thanks to Elaine Chubb, Lisa Graff, Janet Renard, Pam Scordas, Jennifer Unter, Tom Yezerski, and especially my editor, Beverly Reingold, for helping me on this journey, and to Katie McCabe, Christy Smith Treece, and my mother, Willeyne McCune Clemens, who walked every step of *The Winner's Walk* with me.

—NRP

Contents

THE WINNER'S WALK

Applause

Case Callahan looked down and noticed that his hands were red.

It wasn't the brick red of the paint on the stable doors at Callahan Farm, where his family lived between the roll of two hills near Twin Creeks, Virginia. That red greeted him early every morning, when he went with his father to make a breakfast of sweet feed and hay for the show jumpers Mr. Callahan trained there.

It wasn't even the blood red that had almost made Case pass out when one of those horses, Tom Sawyer, had chomped down hard on three of his fingers. That red had gotten Case five stitches and a lesson about the proper way to feed lumps of sugar to a horse: flat on the palm of the hand instead of from the fingertips.

Case's hands were the purplish red that came from clapping too hard, from trying to make his palms pound out a proper round of applause for his mother on her opening night.

He was clapping as hard as he could, watching to see if his mother would smile at him from the stage, where she was bowing low as she held hands with an older man dressed in a white suit. His mother had said she would smile at him, and Case knew she would try to remember. With so many people clapping, though, maybe she would forget again, the way she did last year when she had played Maria in *The Sound of Music*. Case had liked that play better than *The King and I*, tonight's production, but he had never seen his mother look prettier than she did right now, with her hair falling in ringlets over the shoulders of a long, full-skirted dress.

For a few seconds, Case thought his mother might be turning toward him to smile, but the man in front of him stood up and blocked his view. Then Mr. Callahan sprang to his feet, cupping his hands to echo the claps even louder. Case's older sister, Quinn, rose and applauded in long sweeps, her arms high above her head, and Case looked around at people standing for his mother in every corner of the theater. He wondered if all their hands were clapping red, too.

Case stood up, but he was shorter than anyone else around. He had to lean over to see his mother's face.

There was more applause than Case had ever heard—not that he was a stranger to applause. He couldn't remember a time when his family wasn't clapping for one of their own. With his mother a popular actor, his father the favorite for the big show jumper championship again, and Quinn's butterfly stroke recently claiming the blue ribbon in another state swimming meet, Case figured his hands would be plumb worn out from clapping by the time he turned ten.

As Case's family was walking out of the theater, they ran into an old friend. "It's been a great year for the Callahans, hasn't it?" he said.

"I read about one of you in the newspaper almost every week."

Maybe Mom and Dad and Quinn, but not me, Case thought as his father pushed him forward to shake the man's bony hand. *His* name had never been in the newspaper, and nobody had ever had the occasion to clap for *him*. He hoped that would change soon. Over the next month, he would have three chances to become a winner. The spring talent show at his school was coming up in exactly one week; the end-of-year science projects were due the week after that; and Case felt *especially* optimistic about winning the novice jumping class at a junior horse show the first weekend in June. If he was lucky, he, too, might get some applause before long.

Case wished his mother were going home to Callahan Farm with them tonight. If only she could work at home, as his father did. With a little help from part-time stable hands and some from Case and Quinn, his father bred, bought, sold, and trained champion jumpers, all right there at Callahan Farm. They had eleven horses on the farm, not counting Case's pony, Sherlock;

when Scarlett O'Hara foaled in the summer, they'd have a dozen. They also had two prissy cats—no dogs allowed, much as Case wanted one. But for the next four weeks, they wouldn't have his mother there. She would be on tour around the South with the rest of the cast through the last performance. The two weeks she had been away at rehearsals already seemed like two months.

"I'll be home right after school lets out," she promised when she walked with them to the car. He thought about reminding her that she was missing what could be his best month ever, but he didn't want her to feel bad.

"You'll all have so much fun, you won't even realize I'm gone." Case's mother was such a great actor, she could almost make him believe what she said.

Mrs. Callahan hugged Quinn and Case to her for a long time and kissed their father goodbye on the cheek. "Case really needs a haircut," she reminded Mr. Callahan, brushing Case's blond hair away from his eyes before he climbed into the car beside his father. Quinn slid down on the backseat, snapped her seat belt shut, and made herself comfortable for the two-hour trip from Richmond back to Twin Creeks.

Case suddenly wished his father would sing —his mother always did when she was driving. Or tell a funny story. She was good at that, too. Mr. Callahan usually didn't talk much when he drove, and he never, ever sang. Case and Quinn had bet a dollar on the number of words their father would say before they reached Twin Creeks. Quinn chose 200; Case decided to go with 150. Quinn kept the tally on a paper napkin to see who came closest, making a pencil mark for every word Mr. Callahan said.

Every once in a while, Case would turn around and see Quinn mouthing the number to him. They both started to giggle when their father reached 140.

"What's going on?" their father asked. He knew they were up to something.

"Don't say another word, Dad," Case begged. "Not even one."

"I don't suppose you want to tell me why?"

Quinn held up nine fingers, laughing out loud.

"Shhhhh," Case said to his father.

"We made a bet on the number of words you'd say on the drive home," Quinn admitted. "Case bet 150; I bet 200. You're at 152 right now, Dad."

"Please don't say another word," Case begged. "We men need to stick together."

"I love you," said Mr. Callahan, holding up three fingers. "Let's see, that makes 155, not counting what I am saying."

"You're up to 168. Keep on talking," Quinn pleaded.

"We always miss your mom, don't we," Mr. Callahan said. That made 7 more words: 175 in all, to be exact. Right in the middle.

Quinn tried as hard as she could to trick her father into saying just one more word, but Mr. Callahan sat in silence, winking at Case from time to time.

"It's a tie. Nobody won," Quinn said, obviously disappointed. They were coming to the Callahan Farm sign.

"Or maybe we're *both* winners," Case said, grinning. He gave his father a huge high five as they headed up the driveway toward home.

Up in the Air

A week later, Case stared at the poster that his music teacher, Mrs. Wright, had pinned to the backstage curtain. "It's more important to do your best than to be the best!" it said.

Mrs. Wright was his favorite teacher, but she was dead wrong, Case thought. Only a loser would say something like that. It was the kind of thing his parents would say to him, and Case didn't believe one word of it.

He especially didn't want to think about losing today. For months, Case had practiced his juggling for the spring talent show. He had started out with two beanbags about as big and heavy as small apples, tossing one bag from his right hand to his left, the other from left to right, making the bags arc over imaginary spots about eight inches in front of his forehead. Then he had moved on to soft colored balls, then to real baseballs, tossing them higher and higher. First he juggled with two, then three, finally four of them. Sometimes he stood on one foot. When his friends saw him juggle, they all said he was a shoo-in to win the talent show, and Case thought they might just be right. He really was good!

Case wanted to wear the right costume for the talent show and juggle in time to music so his act would be more exciting. He asked his mother about the music when she phoned home. She knew exactly how he should dress, too. He finally decided on "Take Me Out to the Ball Game." Mrs. Wright said she could play it for him on the piano. And he would wear his gray baseball uniform with *Callahan* emblazoned on the back.

Yes, Case thought he really could win. The talent show winner got a gold trophy; it was actually made of plastic, but it looked like real gold. Case could almost see it sitting on his bookshelf right now.

His mother had called to wish him well. His father had given him a lucky horseshoe to carry in his backpack. And Quinn had found him a four-leaf clover in front of their house. He wished his family could be there to see him, but this event was for kids only, since the school auditorium wasn't large enough to hold the students and their parents, too. He'd just have to wait until he got home to show off his trophy.

Mrs. Wright had said that everybody was talented in some way, and anybody who wanted to perform could sign up. Since there hadn't been tryouts for the show—or rehearsals either—Case didn't know how talented his competition was. But he had a good feeling about this. He really did!

Case stood behind the folds of the curtain, watching the school's most talented students scramble onstage as Monica Miller, who was president of the sixth grade *and* captain of the safety patrol, introduced each performer. To be fair, Mrs. Wright had made them draw numbers to determine the order of the acts.

"First, Harry Algabright will perform 'Oh Where, Oh Where Has My Little Dog Gone?'" Monica said cheerfully. Harry lumbered to the microphone, grinning at his friends in the front row as he walked. Everybody in the school knew Harry couldn't sing a note, and he certainly couldn't play any musical instrument. Harry was the most popular boy in the fourth grade and Case's best friend, but even Case had to admit that Harry couldn't do anything well—except burp. He was by far the best burper at Twin Creeks Elementary. Case had heard him try to burp the whole alphabet once during lunch period, and he'd gotten as far as *T-U-V* before his wind gave out.

Harry took a bottle of cola from his coat pocket, twisted off the top, grinned at his friends again, and downed about four swigs without stopping. Then he swallowed a giant gulp of air, bowed at the audience, and began to burp. Case couldn't believe it! His burps really did sound like "Oh Where, Oh Where"—until Mrs. Wright pulled the stage curtain, cutting him off.

And then Case heard Monica say under her breath, "You are disgusting, Harry Algabright, absolutely disgusting!" Case couldn't hear what Mrs. Wright said to Harry, but he could tell from her expression that she, too, thought Harry's act was disgusting.

The boys in the audience loved it. They clapped and hollered and laughed. Then the principal, Mrs. McCormick, stood up and stared at them sternly from behind her wire-rimmed glasses; she wore that stop-it-right-now look every kid knows. The boys got quiet, but Case was sure they were all still laughing inside. He thought that, inside, some of the girls must have been laughing, too. Case wished deep down that he had the nerve to do something like Harry had done, but he knew he didn't.

The Terrific Trio—that's what the three girls called themselves—came next. Two of them played a duet they had learned for their piano recital—probably something by Bach or Beethoven or Brahms, one of those old music guys whose name started with a *B,* Case thought. Their friend danced around the stage in a tight pink leotard while they played. The crowd clapped politely. Case could tell that Monica and Mrs. Wright liked that act much better.

For the next act, Allen Taylor told some old knock knock jokes that everybody knew. When nobody laughed, Case felt sorry for him.

Then it was Case's turn. Mrs. Wright sat down at the piano, which was on the side of the stage. Case walked onstage carrying his catcher's mitt and a baseball cap, hoping nobody could tell how scared he was. When Mrs. Wright began to play, Case relaxed a little. He could almost hear the words to the song running around the bases in his head:

Take me out to the ball game.
Take me out with the crowd.

He put his mitt on the floor, took some base-balls out of his cap, put the cap on his head backwards, and started to juggle. First he juggled three balls. No drops. Not even one. The audience cheered. So far so good, he thought.

Mrs. Wright kept on playing the song.

Buy me some peanuts and cracker jack.
I don't care if I never get back.

She added more piano flourishes with every line. The audience clapped louder as Case tossed one of the baseballs high into the air, so high that it brushed the top of the stage curtain and made it flutter. When he added a fourth baseball, Mrs. Wright really began to pound the piano—so hard he thought the keys might fly off.

Let me root, root, root for the home team.
If they don't win, it's a shame.

Case tossed the four baseballs into the air and watched them make a perfect arc again and again as the crowd cheered louder and louder. It wasn't as much applause as his mother had got-

ten the previous Friday, but it was pretty loud, and it sure sounded good to his ears.

Case had practiced the finale over and over and knew he could do it: throw an extra-high toss, turn around backwards, and catch the last baseball just as the song ended. He could picture the whole audience jumping to their feet, applauding so hard their hands would throb and turn purplish red.

But one of the baseballs strayed loose and bounced—first on the floor, then toward Mrs. Wright's piano.

Case knew things were going wrong when he heard a thud. He was pretty sure he was in trouble when noisy notes crashed from the piano keys. Then he saw Mrs. Wright rubbing the top of her head, where the baseball had landed. Mrs. Wright tried to be a good sport; she scooped up the errant baseball and pitched it back to Case. But Case could tell by the expression on Mrs. Wright's face that the smack had really hurt, and he felt horrible.

The audience sat in silence. Case didn't know what to say or do. He put his baseballs back into his cap and trudged offstage, stopping long enough to tell Mrs. Wright how sorry he was.

"You've ruined the whole talent show!" Monica barked at Case after he had come through the curtain. She looked as mad as a wet hen, as his father would say.

Case knew one thing for sure—he wouldn't be taking home the trophy that day. He was glad that his family hadn't been there to see his humiliation. But Case didn't count himself out yet. This was only the first strike. Maybe he would bring home a trophy for his science project next week.

The last line of the old song rang unplayed in his ears:

For it's one, two, three strikes, you're out,
At the old ball game.

Heart Sounds

Case was pounding out a steady pulse of beats: soft-*hard*, soft-*hard*, soft-*hard*.

Quinn knocked on the door of his bedroom. "What's going on in there?" she shouted. "Let me in."

"I don't have to," Case yelled back. "You're not my mother."

Quinn had crowned herself queen of the house while their mother was on tour, and she never missed a chance to let Case know it. True, she had tried to make him feel better when he told her about the talent show, just the way his mother would have done. But that didn't give his sister the right to boss him around.

Quinn had even taken over the cooking. She'd turned their kitchen into Café Quinn, complete with a weekly menu designed on their computer. She had decided it would be creative to make the dinner start with the same letter as the day of the week.

CAFÉ QUINN
Monday . . . *Macaroni and cheese*
Tuesday . . . *Turkey pot pies*
Wednesday . . . *Wieners and beans*
Thursday . . . *Tomato soup and tuna salad*
Friday . . . *Fish sticks*
Saturday . . . *Spaghetti*
Sunday . . . *Steak*

Case knew the macaroni came straight from a blue box, the pot pies and fish sticks hit the microwave fresh from the freezer, the beans and tomato soup were poured out of cans. That would be fine if Quinn didn't act like a fancy chef on one of those boring cooking shows his mother watched—the ones Case surfed through as fast as he could. Case could hardly wait: tonight was tuna night.

"You better open the door right this instant! If you don't open the door by the time I count to three, I'm going to the stables to get Dad." Quinn sounded like thirteen-going-on-thirty-something—and she meant it.

Case quit pounding at "two" and opened the door.

Quinn stood there and looked into his room, her hands on her hips, shaking her head. "What are you doing now?" She picked up a tiny glass bottle and held it near the light. "Why are you using the red food coloring? I might need it for one of my recipes."

Case couldn't imagine which of her alphabetical delights might need food coloring. Maybe she wanted to make the fish sticks look as if they were bleeding. Bleeding fish sticks. Yum! He started pounding on the mattress. Soft-*hard*. Soft-*hard*. Soft-*hard*. "That's the sound a heart makes," Case said.

Quinn surveyed the floor, her face pinched into a frown. Two old aquariums rested dismantled on top of a plastic cloth that covered the carpet. Modeling clay sat on the floor in fist-sized clumps. An encyclopedia, volume H, lay open near three sheets of poster board and two aquarium pumps with clear vinyl tubing. A small tape recorder whirred quietly nearby.

"Now look what you've done! I've never seen such a mess!" Quinn scolded.

"What I've done is thought of a project that just might win the science fair at school." Case started pounding on his desk again. Soft-*hard*. Soft-*hard*. Soft-*hard*. He stopped to hand her a sketch scrawled on a piece of notebook paper.

"This looks like a blob with four skinny arms," she said, laughing a little.

"For your information, it is a human heart."

"A heart?" She laughed harder.

"Well, it'll be a heart when I get through," Case said calmly. "You'll see when I bring home a blue ribbon."

Case expected her to laugh again, but she didn't. She picked up a lump of clay, then fingered the clear vinyl tubing on the aquarium pumps. He kept pounding, this time on a pillow. Soft-*hard*. Soft-*hard*. Soft-*hard*.

"I want my clay model to make heart sounds, but I can't figure out exactly how to do it," Case admitted. "A real heart goes Lub-*dub*. Lub-*dub*. Lub-*dub*." He pounded on his leg. "Soft-*hard*. Soft-*hard*. Soft-*hard*."

"When's the science fair?" Quinn asked, looking at the picture of a heart in the encyclopedia.

"I've got lots of time to finish this. Harry hasn't even started his project yet."

"You didn't answer my question. I asked you when."

Case thought she sounded just like their mother. "Tomorrow." He felt sheepish.

"Didn't I hear you tell Dad you had your project under control? Didn't I hear you tell Mom the same when she called to remind you?"

He expected Quinn to keep yelling at him, but she didn't. "Looks like you could use some help," she said instead, setting the clay gently on the floor. "I might have time after dinner."

Case pounded on the floor as she left. Soft-*hard*. Soft-*hard*. Soft-*hard*. Lub-*dub*. Lub-*dub*. Lub-*dub*.

When the family had finished eating, Case helped Quinn scoop the rest of the day's tuna salad into a bowl for leftovers and fill the dishwasher while their father went down to the stables for the evening feeding. Case knew Quinn had won the science fair when she was at Twin Creeks Elementary, and he hoped she would think of something to help him win it as well.

Quinn stayed in Case's room late into the evening while he worked. Every so often she left, coming back with Rice Krispies snacks, his favorite, and peanut butter treats, hers.

After Case had shaped the soft clay into a heart the size of his father's fist, he removed the clear tubes and fashioned arteries and veins from them, pressing them into the right places. He filled the tube that led from the heart to the lungs—the pulmonary artery—with water he had tinted dark red, and poured a brighter red liquid into the vein leading from the lungs to the heart. Then he attached both tubes to the aquarium pumps, plugged the pumps into outlets, and watched the fake blood circulate into and out of the heart. Thanks to the two different pumps, the dark red blood seemed to become oxygenated and turn bright red, as if by magic.

At Quinn's suggestion, Case had recorded a toy tom-tom noise while Quinn had drummed it, making a sound a lot like that of a heartbeat.

"You've got first place locked up," his sister assured him when he finished.

In the morning, Mr. Callahan loaded the project into the bed of his pickup truck for the five-mile journey to school. Case noticed that he treated the clay heart as tenderly as a newborn foal, tucking an old horse blanket all around so it wouldn't get smushed.

Case sat his project on a card table in the gym, right between Harry Algabright's and Monica Miller's. Monica had done hers on volcanoes, and Case could tell from her six posters that it was really good. Harry had only a tape recorder and one messy poster on his table, and he wouldn't show the poster to anybody.

Harry whispered to Case, "I have researched gaseous eructation for this project." Case didn't know what that was, but it sounded very important when Harry said it. Case hoped the judges wouldn't find a plain old heart too boring.

They all stood beside their projects, waiting for the three judges to walk by and give them a score. One judge was a doctor; Case thought she might have come straight from a hospital because she was wearing a white coat and had a stethoscope peeking out of her pocket. People with stethoscopes were always smart, Case figured. The other judges also looked smart. One had a bunch of ballpoint pens sticking out of his shirt pocket. Monica guessed that maybe he wrote science books or something. Harry said he was sure the third judge was a teacher; she knew how to give that stop-it-right-now look, too. Mrs. Hurst, the science teacher, and Mrs. McCormick, the principal, were walking with the judges, who stopped at each table, asked questions, and jotted hurried notes.

Harry looked composed when the judges examined his gaseous eructation poster, but Case could tell he was up to something. He turned on the tape recorder and started laughing before it made its first sound. The machine let out a loud belch. Then another. Then a third. Case recognized the tune: "Oh Where, Oh Where," which Harry had tried to burp in the talent show.

The doctor spoke first. "Gaseous eructation is the medical term for burping," she said, looking at the other judges. Case could tell she was trying hard not to laugh. The other judges were trying, too, but even the one who looked like a teacher had a smile puckering her face.

The judges all wore serious expressions, however, as they inspected Harry's poster of symptoms and treatments for gaseous eructation. Case could tell that Mrs. Hurst wasn't happy about Harry's project. "You said we could do anything that interested us," Harry protested as she shut off the tape recorder.

The judges moved down the aisle to Case's project. He turned on his tape recorder, hoping the lub-*dub*s would sound good to the doctor.

Case plugged in the pumps, and the colored water started to move through the vinyl veins and arteries. The doctor took out her stethoscope and pretended to listen to the clay model while the other judges examined Case's posters.

"I thought for a minute you had a real heart there." The doctor winked at him after she said it, and Case thought that was a good sign. He could almost hear Mrs. McCormick announcing his name over the intercom.

The judges were just leaving Case's table when the pulmonary artery broke loose from the pump. Fake blood squirted all over the doctor's white coat, all over Mrs. Hurst's gray hair, all over Mrs. McCormick's pink blazer. It sprayed Monica Miller's erupting volcano dark red, too.

"Now you've ruined the whole science fair," Monica muttered to Case as he tried to mop up all the red stains with the tail of his best white shirt. "Didn't you do enough damage at the talent show?"

That night, Case told his family everything over fish sticks.

"Maybe I should have dried it longer with my hair dryer," Quinn said.

"Maybe the tube worked itself loose when I drove your project to school in my truck," said his father.

Case didn't say so, but he was pretty sure the problem wasn't with the hair dryer, and it wasn't with the truck. Maybe, he thought, he was the only one in his family who was not cut out to be a winner.

So Close

Case had been to lots of horse shows. He had always gone to see his father compete, and he had seen Quinn win shows, too, until swimming practice had started taking up most of her time. This was different. It was the first Saturday in June, and Case himself was in the saddle, number 18 pinned to the back of his black coat.

All winter, his father had taught Case to keep his legs tight to the saddle and let the reins follow his pony's mouth perfectly over the jumps. Night after night, Case had lain awake, imagining his walk to the winner's circle. This wouldn't be like the talent show, he promised himself, or like the science fair either. His mother was coming home next week, after her month on tour, and he wanted to surprise her with a blue ribbon. Case wouldn't, *couldn't*, let this be his third strike.

"Number 18, Case Callahan, is riding Sherlock," the announcer said crisply.

Mr. Callahan patted Sherlock gently on the rump.

"Good luck, Case!" Harry Algabright yelled through cupped hands. He was standing beside Mr. Callahan at the paddock gate.

Case felt confident as he guided his pony through the white gate and into the jumping ring. He and Sherlock had to follow a course set up with a number of obstacles, go over them without knocking anything down, and make complicated turns in just the right way. He cantered a slow circle, then headed straight onto the course.

The first jump was a low brush, and Sherlock soared above it easily. "Good boy," Case said, and they were on their way toward the second one, which was called a chicken coop. Sherlock took off a little early, but cleared it anyway. There wasn't even the tiniest splash at the water jump, and Sherlock took the two single poles called an in-and-out correctly, with only one stride between them.

Case could hear his father cheering him over every obstacle, and Harry, too. Case's pony cantered around the loop toward the last hurdle: a striped horizontal pole two and a half feet off the ground. Case could tell that Sherlock was anxious to clear this one. His canter was turning into a gallop. "Don't rush it," Case heard his father yelling. "Take it easy, son. You're almost home."

Suddenly a fat basset hound lumbered into the ring. He squatted down on his hind legs in front of the last jump and looked around at the crowd with sad eyes. When Case jerked Sherlock's reins to avoid him, Sherlock turned abruptly and Case fell from the saddle, hitting his right arm hard on the pole.

Somehow Case managed to choke down the scream that came to his throat, but he couldn't stop the tears. Case felt the dog licking his face,

then saw Sherlock bending over him and his father kneeling beside him. Harry was right behind them, grabbing Sherlock's reins and holding them tight. Case noticed that his father's big hands were shaking.

Harry stood nearby with Sherlock as two men lifted Case ever so gently onto a stretcher. He could hear the crowd clapping when the men eased him into the ambulance, and he wondered why.

The ambulance siren began to blare after they had headed out of the showgrounds and onto the highway. Case thought he saw tears puddle in the corner of his father's eyes as he sat down beside Case, holding his hand all the way to the hospital.

Instead of a walk to the winner's circle and his first blue-ribbon win, Case got an ambulance ride to the emergency room and a cast for his badly broken arm.

"I came as soon as I could get a flight," Mrs. Callahan said, rushing through the back door the next morning as if there were still an emergency going on. She set her large suitcase on the kitchen floor and gently patted the plaster cast on Case's right arm. Case gave his mother a long hug with his left one, trying hard not to let her know how much his other arm hurt. Mr. Callahan kissed his wife on top of the head while Quinn put down a spatula and rushed to hug her, too.

It was early Sunday morning, and Café Quinn was in full swing. The smell of scrambled eggs, sausages, and sourdough toast welcomed Mrs. Callahan back from Atlanta.

"You didn't have to come home, Mom," Case said, rubbing the plaster cast. He knew that tonight was the last performance of her play, and he hated for her to miss it.

"That's what understudies are for," his mother said. "Tell me what happened."

"I fell off Sherlock at the show yesterday afternoon," Case answered her. He rubbed his cast again. "It didn't hurt all that much. Not really."

"Our son is a hero," Mr. Callahan said.

"I'm no hero." Case denied it softly.

"Well, don't tell that to the McGees. They felt just terrible that their dog, Louis, had gotten loose and caused so much trouble."

Case listened as Quinn told her slightly exaggerated version of the story over breakfast. "Louis kept licking Case's face as he was lying on the ground, waiting for the ambulance—like he was saying he was sorry. You should have seen Case's arm! The broken bone was actually poking Case's skin out," she said. "It was so gross!"

"Sounds like you were lucky," his mother said. She leaned over the table and kissed his forehead lightly. "It could have been a whole lot worse."

Case knew his mother would say something like that to make him feel better. If she had been at home, she probably would have told Case how lucky he was that his stray baseball hadn't knocked Mrs. Wright unconscious and that the spurting artery hadn't drowned the science fair judges. "When a door closes, a window opens," she often liked to say.

But Case didn't think a window would be

opening for him anytime soon. It was only two days after school ended, and what he had thought would be a whole summer of horse shows was already ruined!

After breakfast, Case walked down to the pasture to see Sherlock. It always made him feel better to talk to his pony, who was nosing hay by the gate. Sherlock nudged his muzzle against Case's good arm, begging for a rub.

"We almost won, didn't we, fellow?"

Sherlock nickered at Case's question.

Case felt even worse for Sherlock than he did for himself.

At that moment Case heard a sound—once, twice, three times—coming from the direction of the pond at the end of the pasture. The sound was not too far off, maybe two football fields away. Sherlock must have heard it first; his ears were standing straight up. Case loped toward it, Sherlock right behind. When Case reached the boat dock, he heard it again.

He couldn't believe what he saw straddling the seat of their rowboat. A golden retriever looked up at him with eyes sadder than those of the basset hound that had ruined his day. His coat looked even worse, with burrs matted into a few giant clumps of reddish fur. But there was something about this dog that made Case think he was special. Case longed to take him home.

"Let's go!" Case called. The dog trotted beside Sherlock all the way to the stables, and Case noticed he was limping a little on his front leg. Case reached down and pulled out a prickle stuck in the dog's paw. Case wished he could pick up the dog and carry him the rest of the way, but his broken arm wouldn't let him bear the weight.

"Look what I found!" Case called out.

Mr. Callahan came out of the tack room, leaned down, and rubbed his hands over the dog's ribs. He pried open the dog's mouth.

"You'd better look at his paw, too," Case said, holding it gently. "There was something stuck in it."

"Needs a haircut, doesn't he?" Mr. Callahan said. He went back to the tack room and returned with an electric horse clipper. The dog pricked up his ears at the soft whir of the blade. Ripples of his matted fur fell to the floor.

"Wonder how he got to our boat," Case said.

"He's probably lost. Looks like a purebred golden retriever to me, too good a dog for someone to drop off on a country road."

"He looks like a stray to me. I don't think anybody owns him," Case said, watching for his father's reaction. "We should call him Noah because I found him on a boat." He picked up clumps of fur from the sawdust covering the stable floor and carried them to the trash barrel.

"You think Mom'll let me keep him?" Case asked, now walking toward the house. Noah followed close behind, without a trace of a limp.

"I wouldn't get my hopes up if I were you, son," Mr. Callahan said, winding the cord neatly around the clippers. "I wouldn't get my hopes up."

Finders Keepers

"**I** wish you had stayed on tour!" Case said. It was the closest he had ever come to sassing his mother, and even Quinn gasped at the tone of his voice. Case stormed out the back door, the scrawny dog at his heels.

Mr. Callahan was down at the stables cleaning tack; Case hoped his father hadn't heard his outburst from there.

He also hoped that his words hadn't hurt his mother's feelings. A little maybe, but not too much. No matter how hard he tried, Case just couldn't make his mother understand how important it was for him to have this dog. His father had understood right away. If his mother had still been on tour, he wouldn't have had to ask her if he could keep the dog, and Case knew his father would have said yes. He just knew it!

"What did your mother say?" Mr. Callahan asked when Case walked into the stables. He handed Case a sponge and a mostly finished can of saddle soap. Using his left hand, Case soaked the sponge in a bucket of water, squeezed it out, steadied a set of leather reins as best he could against a stall door, and lathered on soap. Even with a broken arm, Case knew better than to beg off his chores. While his mother was gone, Case had taken over Quinn's chores at the stables so she could take care of the house. He thought that was a fair trade.

"She said that with two cats, eleven horses, one pony, and a foal on the way, we already have enough to take care of around here."

Mr. Callahan smiled. "I thought so. What else?"

"She reminded me about the no-dogs-allowed rule."

"Doesn't sound too hopeful, does it?" Mr.

Callahan bent down and patted the honey-colored dog at Case's feet. He took the clean reins from Case, buckled them to a bridle and bit, and hung them up on the door of the stall belonging to Finn, as in Huckleberry.

Mr. Callahan loved to read, and he had named all the horses after characters in books. Case hadn't read any of those books yet. He hoped Scarlett would have a colt instead of a filly. Then maybe his father would call him something modern—such as Potter, or at least Harry.

"And when I told her she wouldn't have to do anything for the dog, that I would take care of him, she said it would be a big responsibility."

"Did she remind you that you never remembered to feed the fish in your new aquarium?"

"How'd you know?"

"Well, I've known your mother for a while." He put fresh water in a bucket. "Did she find something for the dog to eat?"

"Leftover steak. Mom cut it up into pieces, the way she used to do for me when I was little."

"That's good," Case's father said, stroking the dog's back gently.

"He must have been starving. He wolfed the steak down in one gulp, like he hadn't eaten in a week," Case said.

"He's all bones, that's for sure—but friendliest dog I've seen in a long time. Seems real smart, too. I think this *is* a really good dog, Case! And he doesn't look too bad in a crew cut."

"If Mom just didn't hate dogs . . ." Case let his sentence drift off, unfinished.

"You've got it figured all wrong," said Mr. Callahan. "Your mother doesn't hate dogs at all."

"She acts like she does."

"Your mother had a dog when we got married. A little bit of a thing she called Bitsy. It looked like a big furry rat, but don't ever tell your mother I said so." He laughed. "She loved it like a baby."

"What happened to Bitsy?"

"One of the horses kicked her. Bitsy died instantly. Your mother cried and cried, said she never ever wanted another dog."

"Where did you bury Bitsy?"

"Down in the north pasture, right beside the corn silo. I told your mother that silo would be Bitsy's tombstone—the tallest tombstone in the county."

"Do you think Mom has forgotten Bitsy?"

"No, Case. I think your mother might be so afraid of losing a dog again that she's a little afraid of loving another one."

Case couldn't remember many times when his father had talked to him so seriously. He liked the way his father's voice sounded, deep and calm. He wondered if his father had ever raised that deep, calm voice to his own mother, but he didn't ask.

"You take Noah for a long walk and let me talk to your mother. I'm not saying you can keep Noah. We've got to do our best to find his owner first. But if nobody claims him, well, I'll try to get your mother to change her mind."

"I'd be so good to him," Case said.

"I know you would, son. You've got a real way with animals. They always know when a person likes them."

"How?"

"They can sense it, I guess. They know when you love them, and they know when you need them. This dog's been through a lot. He needs to be needed."

Mr. Callahan closed the door to the barn and headed toward their house. Case wondered if his mother would tell him that Case had sassed her. If she did, then maybe his father would think he didn't deserve to own a dog as good as Noah. He wished he hadn't talked to his mother that way.

Case hadn't been to the corn silo in a long time, but for some reason he wanted to go there now. He was surprised that Noah stayed near his left foot, always stopping when Case stopped, starting when Case started again. He'd never seen a dog do that before. He picked up a stick and threw it as far as he could with his left arm, almost forgetting how much his right one still hurt.

"Fetch, Noah!" Case yelled. The retriever brought the stick back quickly and laid it at Case's feet.

Case walked around the silo, looking closely

at the ground, then up at the tallest tombstone in Twin Creeks, maybe even in the whole county. He tried to guess where Bitsy might be buried. It made him sad to think of his mother crying her heart out over her dog. He had seen her cry only once. That was in a play, though, so he didn't think it really counted. He wondered if his mother might be crying right now, thinking that her son wished she were still off somewhere acting in a play instead of at home.

Case saw a blur in powder pink racing toward the silo. He knew it must be Quinn, even though she was far off. His sister had more powder-pink outfits than Case cared to count. He couldn't figure out for the life of him why she needed so many clothes. If his mother would let him, he would wear the same long-sleeved baseball shirt every day.

He loped with Noah toward the powder pink. Case knew Quinn must have something important to tell him. She always liked to know things first.

"I overheard Mom and Dad talking, and this is the deal." She tried to catch her breath.

"Mom said you *can* keep the dog—*just* until we find its real owner—*but* he *can't* come in the house." She was still panting. "*And* you have to make posters to put up around town."

"And what if nobody claims Noah? What then?"

Quinn stroked Noah under the chin. "Mom and Dad were speaking real low. I thought they might be talking about how much trouble you're in, so I put my ear up to their door to find out. But they were just talking about the dog." She paused as if she was disappointed. "I couldn't hear everything, but I think Mom might actually be softening. I don't know why, though, considering the way you talked to her."

Quinn acted as if she had never said or done anything wrong in her whole life. Case wanted to tell his sister that snooping on their parents' conversation was almost as bad as sassing, but he decided not to.

He hoped Quinn had heard right. And he hoped more than anything that Noah's real owner would never show up.

Unbelievable!

"**N**ow look what you've done!" Quinn yelled at Case as she picked up one of the pages their printer was spitting out. Quinn had offered to help, but Case had insisted on making the DOG FOUND flyers himself. Case thought that having to make flyers for a dog you wanted to keep felt like a punishment. He hadn't even done anything wrong lately, except sass his mother. His parents had already given him a stern talking-to for that.

"Give that back!" he demanded, grabbing the collar of Quinn's powder-pink polo shirt as she ran back into the kitchen. "It's mine!"

"I can't wait to tell Mom and Dad what

you've done," she said before Case could wrestle the paper away. Then she started reading his flyer out loud in a high-pitched, mocking voice:

"DOG FOUND
One old dog
Black with white spots
Missing one leg
Tail cut off
Barks all the time
Bites people, especially kids
Not very smart
Call 555-0116

"No wonder you wanted to make the flyers yourself! Did you think you could actually get away with this?" she asked. She held the paper high above her head and laughed as Case strained to reach for it.

"I was just experimenting," Case said, embarrassed.

"You made a few mistakes here." Quinn pointed to the words on the page. "The dog's camel-colored, not black. Last time I counted he had four legs, not three." She started laughing. "No spots on him at all. Wouldn't even bite at a horsefly." She laughed louder. "I haven't heard him bark yet, he's got the longest tail I've ever seen, and he seems pretty smart to me." She handed the flyer back to Case. "Other than that, you got everything else right." She laughed so hard her eyes were watering. "Except our phone number. You got that wrong, too. Not that anybody would ever call us to find a dog like that."

"I was just fooling around. I'm too old to think I could get away with something like that!"

"Sounds like you ought to name this dog No Account instead of Noah."

"Very funny, Quinn."

"You better get those flyers finished before Mom and Dad get home—and no more fooling around, if you know what's good for you."

"You are not my mother!" Case said to Quinn, as he did at least once a day.

Case went to the back door and opened it. Noah was waiting for him, head resting on the bottom step. Case scratched the dog's closely cropped shoulders, thinking how embarrassed

Noah must be with such a funny-looking haircut. He wondered where Noah had lived before,
if he missed his old owner, if he was scared nobody would want him.

"Come on in, Noah." Noah hesitated, as if he
knew he should stay outside. "It's okay. Mom's
out doing errands for a while. She won't find
out." Noah wagged his tail and sniffed around
the kitchen. The dog seemed to know he had
found a home.

"You know what Mom said," Quinn reminded him loudly. "The dog's supposed to stay
outside." She took a glob of powder-pink icing
and smoothed it in swirls over a still-warm cake.

Case went back to the family room and sat
down at the computer, not so anxious to work
on the flyers anymore. Noah pillowed his head
on Case's tennis shoe.

The phone rang. "Answer that, Case. I'm
busy—unless it's for me," Quinn said.

Case kept pecking on the computer keys.
"Case, I told you to answer that!" The phone
stopped ringing. When Case looked down,
Noah was standing near him with the phone's

receiver between his teeth. "Would you look at that!" Case exclaimed.

"Look at what?" the voice on the phone questioned. Case recognized his mother's voice and had to think quickly. He looked over the breakfast bar separating the family room from the kitchen and saw the cake. "The icing on Quinn's cake looks like it's made of bubble gum. That's all." He hoped his mother would believe him. "You should see it, Mom. It's gross."

"I'll see the cake when I get home, honey. Are you finished with the flyers yet? Your father said he'd drive you around town to put them up."

"I'm finished with them. Almost."

"Your father went by the vet's when I was at the grocery store. Nobody knew anything about the dog."

Case reached down and rubbed Noah's ears. He felt a little better when he heard that.

"Then he stopped by the pound."

His mother paused, and Case could feel his heartbeats quicken. "Has anyone reported a lost dog?" He tried to act as if the answer didn't matter all that much.

"Not yet. The man said if nobody claimed him within seven days, they'd put him up for adoption. Until then, I guess he can stay."

Seven days. If they could only make it through seven days, Case knew his father would talk his mother into keeping the dog. His father would know just what to say.

"We'll be home in a little while."

"Okay."

Case could hardly wait to hang up the phone. He ran to the kitchen. "You're not going to believe this, Quinn, but Noah answered the telephone."

"Was that before or after he turned black and grew white spots?"

"It's true, Quinn. Noah picked up the phone when it rang and brought it to me in his teeth."

"Do you really expect me to believe that, Case? Go finish those flyers and get that dog out of the house right this minute." Noah looked up and whimpered softly.

"You can stay, Noah. We don't have to pay attention to Quinn," Case said. He walked back to the computer and pointed to a spot near the desk; Noah lay down, his head on Case's foot again.

When the printer finally whirred out another piece of paper, Case held it up to the ceiling light and wished it weren't so perfect. Then he printed twenty more copies. He walked toward the kitchen and stacked the flyers on the counter. Suddenly the family room darkened a little behind him. He looked back at Noah, who was nosing at the light switch.

"Hey, Quinn. Noah just turned out the light."

"Was that before or after he lost his tail?" Quinn said as Case entered the kitchen.

"I'm serious, Quinn. You've got to believe me!" Case said. "Noah must be a trick dog. Maybe he escaped from a circus or something."

Quinn rolled her eyes. Then she put a cover over the cake and headed toward her room.

Case set a bowl of dog food on the kitchen floor. Noah waited patiently in front of it, looking up. "It's okay, fellow," Case said quietly. "Go ahead and eat." Noah licked the edges of the food first; then he gobbled the rest until the food was gone.

After Case had downed a glass of chocolate milk, he opened the dishwasher and looked for an empty space. At that moment Noah took his empty bowl to the open dishwasher and laid it gently on the bottom rack.

"Quinn! Come quick!" Case yelled. "Noah put his bowl in the dishwasher."

"Oh, Case," Quinn called from her room, sounding exasperated. "I don't know what we'll ever do with you. You're absolutely unbelievable!"

Jumping for Joy

"**Y**ou can't peek, Mom. It's a surprise."

Case was glad his mother had finally come home from rehearsing for the Fourth of July pageant she was directing at the Twin Creeks Women's Club. As soon as her white van had rounded the curve to Callahan Farm, he had sprinted from the stables to meet her. Noah had galloped along beside him.

By now, the week's wait to find Noah's owner was long over. At first Case had thought his mother was too busy with the pageant to remember when the seven days were up. Then he'd noticed a leather collar she had brought home from the hardware store with *Noah Callahan* engraved on it, and Case knew Noah was there to stay.

"I have to show you something down at the stables, Mom."

"Has Scarlett foaled early?" Mrs. Callahan guessed. She put her hands over her eyes, and Case steered her past the long red horse trailers with the Callahan Farm logo stenciled on the sides in white. He tried to steady her with his body as she stumbled blindly past the neatly stacked bales of hay, past the freshly painted paddock fence, past the sparkling clean water trough.

"Better than that!" Case replied. "We're almost there."

Case was glad Scarlett hadn't foaled while his father was away at another horse show. His father had taught him what to do if everything went right with the birthing and to have his mother call the vet if anything went wrong. Still, Case was relieved that the old roan mare had decided to wait until his father was home. There had been enough for him to do around the farm without a new foal to take care of.

He led his mother down the aisle that separated two rows of spotless stalls, all sporting brass nameplates. Atticus. Scout. Jem. Tom Sawyer. Huckleberry Finn. Scarlett. Jo March. Gatsby. Oliver Twist. Silas Marner. Mr. Chips. Sherlock.

Mr. Callahan was standing by the jumping ring. Quinn had hitched her horse to the fence and was waiting there, too. "Just a minute, Mom. We're almost ready."

Case and Noah had left Mrs. Callahan leaning against the ring until it was time for her to open her eyes. "Okay, you can open them now!" he hollered.

"I don't see anything," she said, looking around, obviously puzzled. "The jumps are just a little shorter than usual. That's all I see."

"Well, look at this!" Case trotted out to the gate.

"Come on, boy," he called to Noah, and

pointed to a brush jump almost as tall as his own waist. Noah sailed over it, clearing the tops of the cedar branches with inches to spare. Then Noah ran right beside Case as he pointed to the other jumps: over the wall . . . over the striped poles . . . over the in-and-out. He took another wall in stride and headed toward a triple bar, with its three poles wider than Case could stretch out his one good arm.

Noah stopped in front of a white chicken coop. "Go on, Noah!" Case yelled, waving the dog on with his left hand. "Climb it, boy!" The dog scaled one side of the white coop and scrambled down the other. After he'd hurdled two more striped poles and a fence, they both wound down to a stop. Case was a little out of breath, but he tried not to show it. Noah wasn't even panting.

Case felt proud of how graceful Noah had looked, how he had tucked his front legs beneath him just right and had wagged his tail over every jump. "Give me five, Noah," Case said. The two leaped into the air at the same

time, as Case slapped at Noah's front paws playfully with his left hand. Then Case threw a ball
into the middle of the ring, and Noah hurdled
the brush jump again to bring it back.

"Well, would you look at that!" Mrs. Callahan
grinned. She smoothed her hair away from her
face. "I wouldn't have believed it if I hadn't seen
it with my own eyes."

Noah seemed to know she was talking about
him. He brushed up against her skirt, waiting
for a love pat. Mrs. Callahan wrinkled his floppy
ears in her hands and rubbed his head. "I hadn't
noticed the scar under his ear before," she said.
"It looks like a tiny horseshoe."

"Some people think a horseshoe brings good
luck," said Case.

"Isn't Noah amazing?" Quinn asked, knowing
what her mother's answer would be.

"No more amazing than his teacher!" Mrs.
Callahan said.

Case could tell that she was proud. She tried
to hug Case to her, and she ran her soft fingers
through his mop of blond hair. He was afraid

she might even want to kiss his cheek, but he wormed away before she could do it.

"It wasn't that hard to teach him," Case said modestly. "I did it the way Dad trains his horses. We started with low poles at first. He seemed to know what jump he was supposed to take, just by my calling out to him. I guess he's a born jumper." Case had heard his father say that about a few of his best horses. "We wanted to surprise you."

"Case has a way with animals," Mr. Callahan said, smacking a riding crop gently against his tall leather boot. "Go on, son. Tell your mother the rest."

"Dad says this weekend there's a show in Albemarle County for kids and their dogs that jump. He's going to take Noah and me."

"A show for jumping dogs?"

"It's called an agility trial," Mr. Callahan said. "Kind of like show jumping for horses, except you're running beside the animal instead of riding on top." He swatted at a fly with his crop.

"Sounds like fun, Case," his mother said. "You can see how well the other dogs jump, and maybe you and Noah could be *in* a show later this summer when your arm's better."

"We're not going to watch the show," Case said confidently. "We're going to win it."

"But your arm's still in a cast," Mrs. Callahan protested.

"I point with my left hand," Case said. "And I run beside Noah and yell out the names of jumps. Noah knows what he's supposed to do just by hearing my commands."

"Do you think they're ready?" Mrs. Callahan asked her husband.

"Can't hurt to try," Mr. Callahan said. "I've been watching them all morning. Noah can read Case's mind, and he's faster than a rabbit." He swatted at the fly again. "Beats anything I've ever seen."

"Think you and Quinn could come with us?" Case asked his mother. "Harry can't come because he's at the beach."

"I've got pageant rehearsal in the morning, and Quinn's got swim practice for the state meet. But we'll get there somehow."

Case wanted to hug his mother right there.

His father, too. Even Quinn. But instead, he ran with his dog out behind the stables. And there, where nobody could see them, he and Noah gave each other high fives at least twenty times.

The Land of Blues

Case thought that the ring at the agility trial looked a lot like the one at the horse show where he had broken his arm. The jumps were the same, just not as tall. Case knew Noah could fly over them.

But this ring had some things a horse show didn't have: a teeter-totter for the dogs to climb, a tunnel for them to run through, twelve poles to weave themselves around, a tall bridge for them to walk across. There was also a little table for the dogs to wait on top of for five seconds, until the handler gave them the go-ahead to finish the course.

Case had never seen obstacles quite like those before. But Mr. Callahan said that since Case and Noah had come this far, it couldn't hurt to try. "It will be good practice for next time."

When he went to a horse show, Mr. Callahan seemed to know just about everybody, and just about everybody knew him. Here nobody knew Case's father. Case hoped nobody would recognize Noah either. Not that it would matter really. The time to find his owner was up long ago. Noah was Case's dog now.

The woman at the registration table handed Case the number 21, and his mother stuck it to the front of his white shirt. Case hadn't been sure what handlers at agility trials were supposed to wear, since he'd never been to one before. At horse shows, everybody wore special clothes. Here, people were running around the course in jeans and T-shirts and plain old tennis shoes.

Since he'd never shown Noah in a trial before, Case had registered for the beginners class, which had the easiest course. He watched twenty dogs wind their way around the course, the judge's hand signaling when a dog made a mistake. Some knocked poles down. Some took the wrong jump and left the ring without finishing. One dog made a mess on the course, and he had to leave, too.

"Some of those dogs are really fast," Case told Noah, who seemed to understand what Case was thinking. But I'm even *faster*, Noah seemed to say with his eyes, his long tail beating propeller-like against Case's leg.

"Twenty-one on deck!" a man with a whistle called out.

Case looked at his father. "You'll do fine, son," Mr. Callahan said, giving his shoulder a hard squeeze.

"Break a leg," his mother said. That was what actors told each other—it just meant good luck—but after what had happened to him at the horse show, Case didn't want to think about breaking a leg or anything else.

Quinn hugged him and gave Noah a quick pat. Then it was time for them to go.

Case ran beside Noah toward the first set of

jumps. No problem, Noah seemed to say, shaking his tail as he cleared each pole by a foot. "Tunnel," Case called, crossing in front of Noah on the other side of the jump. Noah ran ahead, storming in one side and out the other. "Climb it!" Case shouted as Noah scaled something that looked like a tall A-frame. "Now walk it!" Case yelled, nearing the bridge-like dog walk. Noah beat him to the other end. "Tire!" Case ordered, running toward the red-and-white tire swinging from a stand.

I can do that, too, Noah seemed to say.

Noah had to climb up onto the short table next and lie down for five seconds. "Five, four, three, two, one!" Case counted out loud as Noah waited patiently.

Then Case pointed Noah to another tunnel and a few more jumps, and they were finished. No wayward baseballs. No bleeding hearts. No interfering basset hounds. He and Noah had made it to the finish line! Case gave Noah a turkey treat.

Other dogs had finished the course with-

out making any mistakes either. The fastest one would win.

"Fifty-eight seconds!" a woman looking at the hand of her watch said. "Under a minute! That's quite a run, young man." Case smiled and gave Noah another turkey treat.

"That's some dog you have there," a man with a big camera said to him as Case was waiting for the scores to be posted. "Mind if I take a picture for the newspaper?"

Mr. Callahan nodded his okay. Case sat down beside Noah and grinned at the camera. He was glad Noah looked fatter than he had a few weeks before.

"We'd like to have a copy of that picture, too," Mr. Callahan said, handing the man a business card with his address on it. "Will ten dollars do?"

"Perfect," the photographer said. Then he asked Case a few questions about Noah and jotted his answers in a little notebook. "Would you spell your name, please," he said. "I want to make sure we get it right in the newspaper."

Case was so busy spelling that he didn't understand the announcement. "You and Noah came in first, Case!" Quinn shouted. "Did you hear that? You're the winner!"

Case's family clapped loudly as he picked up the blue ribbon, with Noah right beside him. The ribbon felt smooth in his hand. He tucked it underneath Noah's collar and walked back ringside, where he knew his family would still be clapping.

When they got home that night, Mrs. Callahan said Noah could sleep in Case's room. Case snuggled him, waking up every now and then to give his shoulders a sturdy pat and his big old head a rub.

A Time to Talk

It was almost ten when Case and Noah woke up the next morning. Case pulled on his jeans in a hurry. His father must have fed the horses without him, Case thought. He wondered why his father hadn't whistled him awake, the way he always did.

When he walked into the kitchen, his blue ribbon was draped across the counter, waiting to be hung. Case let Noah out the back door and went to hug his mother. He thought her eyes looked red, as if she had been slicing onions, but the kitchen didn't smell oniony.

Mr. Callahan came into the kitchen and

washed his hands at the sink. His face looked drawn, and Case wished he were smiling, the way he was when Noah had won the blue ribbon yesterday.

"Sit down, son," he said, pointing to a chair. "Your mother and I need to talk to you."

Case couldn't imagine what he had done to make his father frown and his mother cry.

"I wish I didn't have to tell you this, Case, but a man who thinks he might be Noah's owner phoned the house this morning. He wants us to call him back."

Case didn't know what to say. He just sat there, staring at his father, listening to himself breathe. He wished the tile floor would split wide open and swallow his father's words. He went to the door to let Noah in and felt Noah's bushy tail brush against him. "Do we have to?" Case asked quietly. He knew the answer before his father nodded.

"I'll dial the number and talk to him first," Mr. Callahan said. "Why don't you go into the family room and get on the other phone. I want you to hear for yourself what he has to say."

Still wagging his tail, Noah followed Case through the door. Case sat at the desk and picked up the phone. He listened to the ringing. His heart was pounding through his T-shirt, and a pain nibbled at his insides. Quinn came in and pulled up a chair beside him. She patted his cast gently; she looked worried, too.

"Is Bart Woodson there? This is Jack Callahan calling."

"Just a minute," the woman who answered said pleasantly. "He'll be so happy to hear from you." Her voice was high and kind.

"Thanks for calling, Jack." Mr. Woodson cleared his throat. "My wife saw the picture of your son in the Charlottesville paper this morning and thought the dog with him looked a lot like one we lost three months ago. When we read the story about how your son had found him, we decided to give you a call. You were the only Callahan in Twin Creeks, so it wasn't too hard to find your number."

Mr. Callahan didn't say anything. Mr. Woodson kept on talking. "Can you tell me if the dog has a scar under his right ear, one that looks a little like a horseshoe?"

"My son, Case, is on the other phone. He'll tell you."

Case wanted to say no. That there wasn't any scar at all. That the dog Mr. Woodson had lost must be somewhere else. Then it would be all over. He could keep Noah, and nobody would ever know. But he couldn't make himself lie.

"There is a scar; it might look a little like a horseshoe," he said instead, picking up Noah's ear and looking again to be sure. Case's voice was quivering, and he was afraid he might start to cry. He didn't want to, not with his father on the other phone, not with his sister right beside him.

"Now, don't worry, son," Mr. Woodson said, as if he had understood Case's quiver. "We've got another dog now. His name's Gabriel, and he's a golden retriever, too. I'm not asking you to give the dog you found back to us—not after he's been gone so long. We're just relieved to know he's got a good home."

Case couldn't believe what he was hearing. His breathing slowed, and he didn't think his voice would quiver so much anymore.

"What can you tell us about him?" Mr. Callahan asked.

"Well, we named him Duke, after my favorite college basketball team. I have a twelve-year-old daughter named Meg. She uses a wheelchair to get around, and Duke was her service dog. He helped her do absolutely everything. He was kind of like a partner with paws." Mr. Woodson sounded as if he laughed a lot. "Best-trained dog I've ever seen," he said, "although Meg's new buddy, Gabriel, is a close second."

So that explained it, Case thought. Noah had been trained to help people, to be their partner with paws.

"Where did you get Noah, I mean Duke?" his father asked.

"We bought him from a professional dog trainer who had been working with him for almost a year." Mr. Woodson paused. "Duke can perform a hundred tasks, maybe more. Why, he can help a person do almost anything."

Case couldn't believe it. He wondered what Noah could do that he hadn't seen.

"Meg had to go to school with her mom to learn how to work with Duke. How long did you stay, honey? A couple of weeks, wasn't it?" Mr. Woodson listened for his wife's reply. "My wife says two weeks. And then the trainer came to our home, just to be sure Meg and Duke made a good match. We had to go through the same thing with Gabriel—not that we're complaining. We were lucky enough that we could afford to buy one service dog, let alone two. They don't come cheap."

Case wondered how much they had paid for Noah, but he didn't ask. Did Noah cost as much as one of his father's horses? More?

"Some organizations train dogs for free, but people who need them often have to wait five or six years," Mr. Woodson said. "Meg would be in college by then." He cleared his throat again. "There are so few good service dogs out there, and so many people who need them."

"How did you lose Duke?" Case asked.

"Someone stole him right out of our yard.

We had gone to a friend's house for dinner and thought Duke might like to take off his service vest and run around outside while we were gone. Our fence was tall and solid, and we never dreamed someone would cut the padlock and steal our dog. It was a really rotten thing to do."

"I wonder how he got all the way to Twin Creeks," Mr. Callahan said.

"I have no idea," Mr. Woodson said. "I just hope that before he got away, Duke bit the person who stole him on the backside."

Case looked down at Noah. He couldn't imagine Noah biting anybody. He couldn't imagine anybody being mean enough to steal a dog from Meg, either.

His father thanked Mr. Woodson for telling them about the dog. Case thanked him, too. He had never talked to anyone who seemed nicer. He hoped he could meet Meg and Gabriel someday, Mr. and Mrs. Woodson, too.

Homecoming

"**H**oly cow!" Case exclaimed as his father navigated their car down the tree-lined driveway to the Woodsons' home. "It's the biggest house I've ever seen! It's as big as the White House!"

"Just about," Mr. Callahan said. For most of the two-hour drive from Twin Creeks, Noah had been sleeping soundly between the two of them, his head on Case's knee. At the crunch of gravel on the Woodsons' driveway, he sprang to attention and began to look out the window. He whined with excitement.

"Oh, Dad! I think Noah remembers." Case's wonder turned to worry. "Maybe we shouldn't have come here." Noah slapped his tail against Case's face. "Maybe Noah will want to stay."

"It was your idea to come here, son. You can change your mind." Case thought for a moment that his father actually wanted him to, but he couldn't be sure. "We can still turn around."

"What if Mr. Woodson sees how much Meg misses Noah and decides to keep him? He couldn't do that, could he?"

"Seemed to me like a man who would stick to his word."

Noah whimpered even louder as they came to a stop in the middle of a circular driveway.

"Maybe Noah liked living at this place better than at our house." Case looked around at the tennis court on one side. "I wouldn't mind living here." The Callahans' house wasn't nearly as large, and Case hoped he hadn't hurt his father's feelings by making such a big deal about the size of the Woodsons'.

"We can go back home."

"Meg would be disappointed," Case said. He wondered if people who lived in big houses were different from people who didn't, but he didn't dare ask. "Let's not stay too long, though, okay?" he said instead.

"Okay."

Noah was wriggling so hard that Case was afraid he'd jump out the open window. He bounded up the steps first. "Sit, Noah," Case commanded quietly. Noah squatted on his haunches immediately, but he sure didn't seem to feel like sitting. Case wanted Noah to be on his very best behavior when he saw the Woodsons again.

"Take off your ball cap," Mr. Callahan reminded Case. "I'd hate for the Woodsons to think Noah has better manners than you do."

His father didn't really look comfortable, standing on the steps of that big house, waiting to meet the Woodsons. He shifted from one foot to the other. Noah kept his sit, but it was squirmier than usual.

The door opened. A dog wearing a yellow vest was pulling at a strap on the door handle with his teeth. "Good boy, Gabriel," a girl in a wheelchair said kindly, rolling to a stop just in front of them. A man in a polo shirt and a

woman wearing pink pants and a flowery blouse came to the door. Case knew Quinn would like those pants. Noah whimpered loudly and squirmed right out of his good sit.

"We couldn't wait for the three of you to get here," Mr. Woodson said. "Meg has been especially anxious, haven't you, honey?" He bent down, kissed his daughter on the top of her head, and wheeled her chair out of the way. "Come on in."

Mr. Woodson shook Mr. Callahan's hand, then looked at Case's cast. "I broke it at a horse show," Case said, answering Mr. Woodson's unasked question. Then he stuck out his left hand.

Noah seemed to know that he had been invited, too. He ran past the other dog, not even stopping for a sniff, and put his head in Meg's lap. "Oh, Duke," Meg said. "You remember how to say hello, don't you." Meg had trouble making her hand reach out to pet him. "I thought I'd never see you again."

Case was afraid the dog that had opened the door might growl, or even bite Noah, but he didn't. He went calmly to the left side of the wheelchair. "Gabriel, you can say hello," Meg said. Gabriel put his head on the other side of Meg's lap. "Give me kisses," she said. Noah licked Meg on the right cheek over and over and over. Gabriel licked her left one.

"That was cool, the way your dog opened the door for us," Case told Meg. He knelt down beside her chair, stroking Noah's head. Noah lavished big licks on both of his cheeks. "How'd he do that?"

"I just said *door*," Meg explained proudly. "Duke used to do that for me. I bet he hasn't forgotten."

For a minute, Case had to remember who Duke was. Noah picked up his ears at the sound of his old name. "Door, Duke," Meg said, lifting her limp hand slightly and pointing toward the door.

Noah turned first to Case, who nodded his okay. The dog turned around and headed back to the front door, pulling on the strap to the handle gently. "Would you look at that, Dad!" Case exclaimed.

"Don't tell me Noah already wants to go back to Twin Creeks," said Mrs. Woodson, smiling. "You just got here."

"I know he's glad to see you all," Mr. Callahan said. He kept shifting his weight from foot to foot. "He almost jumped out of the car when we stopped."

"Why don't we all go out on the sunporch," Mrs. Woodson suggested. Meg led the way down the hall, Gabriel beside the wheelchair. They walked past poster-size oil portraits on the walls. Case wondered if one of the pictures might be of Meg, painted when she was about his age. She was sitting on a velvet bench, her hands folded neatly in her lap, feet crossed at the ankles.

"That's me before I had the skiing accident," Meg said.

Case wanted to tell her about his accident, but a broken arm seemed small compared to what had happened to her. She looked beautiful in the portrait, with her blond hair falling softly around the dimples on her cheeks. He thought she still looked beautiful.

They followed Meg through the dining room. Case could almost see himself in the dining room table, it was waxed so shiny. He had never sat at a table that long, with eight chairs on each side. How many people could be in Meg's family if they needed a table that big? Did all the people in those portraits come for Christmas dinner?

Meg and Gabriel led them into a bright room at the back of the house. Case saw lots of leafy plants and white wicker chairs to sit on.

"Want to go outside?" Meg asked before Case could sit down.

He could tell she wanted to. "Sure."

"Door," Meg said. Gabriel nudged the screen door open with his nose, and Case and Meg and Noah followed him onto a brick patio. Mr. Callahan sat with the Woodsons in the sunroom.

All in a Day's Work

Case couldn't believe what he saw: a swimming pool in the shape of a lima bean. Near the diving board stood a long building with a dressing room on each end. Case noticed an alcove with a sink and a small stainless-steel refrigerator in the middle, and lots of glasses on the shelves above the sink.

"Want something to drink?" Meg asked, looking toward the fridge. "I do."

"I'll get you something," Case offered.

"Gabriel can get it," Meg said proudly. "Fridge, Gabriel." The dog trotted toward the refrigerator, tugged on the strap fastened to the handle, and took a bottle of root beer in his teeth. He came toward them. "Give it." Gabriel put the bottle in Meg's lap. "Good boy," she said.

"Why don't you ask him to get you one?" she suggested.

"Do you think Noah can do that?"

Meg nodded. "He used to be really good at it. I could even tell him what kind of drink I wanted. He never made a mistake." She paused. "I don't think a dog ever forgets, do you?"

"Fridge, Noah," Case said. Noah got up from the deck of the pool, went toward the refrigerator, opened the door by the strap, brought Case a root beer, and went back to the refrigerator to push the door shut.

Meg struggled to twist the top off the bottle.

"Let me open that," Case said finally, straining his face and screwing the bottle cap off with his left hand. "They sure put those tops on tight, don't they?" he said, hoping Meg wouldn't feel bad about needing his help.

Case noticed how long it took for Meg to get

the bottle of soda to her lips. He wanted to hold it up for her, but she seemed determined to do it herself.

They were quiet for a while, and Case suddenly wished he were more like his mother. She would know what to say. She always knew what to say when nobody else was talking. "What else can Gabriel do?" Case felt the fizz of root beer tickle his throat.

"He carries my notebooks in his saddle bags and picks up my pencils if I drop them at school. Dad calls him my gofer. He can pick up lunch money if I drop it, even something as small as a dime."

Case fumbled in his pocket and found a dime. "Prove it," he said. He put the dime on the tile around the pool.

"Get it!" Meg commanded. Gabriel walked toward the dime. Holding it in place with his paw, he used his nose to nudge the coin to its rim, picked it up in his teeth, and carried it back to Meg.

Case shook his head. "I can't believe it. What else can he do?"

"He helps me make my bed."

"No way!"

"He really does. Mom throws a sheet on the middle of the bed and Gabriel pulls the corners over the mattress. Then he pulls the covers up over the pillows."

Could Noah help him make his bed? Could Noah get the corners of the sheets to fit tighter than he could? One of the corners always pouffed out when Case did it. He couldn't wait to see if Noah could do it better when they got home.

"Once I was trying to get something out of a drawer, and I spilled all of my bracelets on the floor," she said, laughing. "Gabriel picked them up one by one and put them back in the drawer."

"No way!"

"Really!"

"And one time Gabriel beat Mother at bowling. Almost bowled a hundred. He pushed the ball down the alley for me with his nose." She laughed again. Meg had the prettiest smile Case had ever seen. "Mom's still mad about that. We had bet a dollar."

"You mean Gabriel can even go to bowling alleys?" Case had never heard of a dog in a bowling alley before.

"He can go everywhere with me. The kids at school are crazy about him. So are the teachers."

"To church?"

"Every Sunday."

"Out to eat?"

Meg nodded. "There's a law that says he can."

"Noah can do cool stuff, too," Case said quietly.

"I know," said Meg. "He used to do cool stuff for me. He can do everything Gabriel can."

"But I taught him some new stuff myself. Want to see?" Case knew it was wrong to show off, but he wanted Noah to feel important, too.

He looked around the pool. "Should I ask your folks if I could borrow those wastebaskets for a few minutes? And maybe that long pole with the net on the end of it? There's a broom. I could use that if they wouldn't mind. How about that lounge chair? I'll need that little table, too."

"They won't mind," Meg said.

Case ran around the pool, setting up his jumping course. He steadied the long pole on top of two small wastebaskets and the broom between two chairs. He turned a lounge chair on its side. Then he took five baskets bulging with petunias and placed them in a long row, the rims of their pots almost touching. "Pretend it's a jumping course," Case told Meg. "Noah's a jumping champion. He won an agility trial last week."

"I know. Dad showed me his picture in the newspaper."

"Well, here goes," said Case, pointing to the first makeshift hurdle. "Jump, Noah." Noah sailed over the broomstick easily, clearing it by at least a foot. Case pointed to the lawn chair. "Jump." Another hurdle cleared. Noah headed for the pole with the net used to clean the pool. "Jump," Case said. "Big jump," he called as Noah sprinted toward the flowerpots, not even touching the petals on his way over them. Case pointed to a short, square table. "Table!" he shouted. Noah jumped on top of the table. "Down." Noah hunkered close to the tabletop. Case counted the seconds: "Five, four, three, two, one." Then he gave Noah another command. "Off!"

"High five!" Case called to Noah after he leaped off the table. Noah stood on his hind legs, touching Case's hand playfully with his paws.

"I'll do even better when my cast comes off." At once he wished he hadn't said that. He wondered if Meg's arms would ever get better, or if Gabriel would always have to be her arms and her legs.

"You taught him to jump like that?" Meg asked.

Case had to admit to himself that the jumping had been pretty impressive. "Sure did," he said, moving closer to Meg. "All by myself. I've got a way with animals. Dad says so."

"I say so, too." Meg struggled to push a button and wheeled her chair closer to Noah, Gabriel right beside her. "Do you think you could teach Gabriel to jump like that? I couldn't run beside him, like you do, but maybe I could figure a way to let him know which jump to take."

"I can teach Gabriel," Case said, full of confidence. "I know I can. We'll figure out something so he'll know which jump you mean."

Meg sat smiling, squinting her eyes in the sun, while Case put everything back exactly where he'd found it.

"Brace!" Meg said then. Noah got to her first. He stood beside her as she struggled to lift her body out of the chair and leaned against him. She walked ever so slowly toward the water, using his strong shoulder to balance herself. Then, ever so slowly, she sat down.

Case sat down beside her and took off his tennis shoes, kicking up water with his feet. Noah pulled off both of Meg's shoes by the heels. Then she dangled her legs in the water, too.

"I bet you wish Noah still lived with you," Case said, splashing a little water her way. He waited for her answer, afraid that he knew what it would be. He splashed water back at Noah and Gabriel while he was waiting for her to talk.

"I wish he'd never been stolen," Meg said. "But then I would never have met Gabriel."

"I bet you'd like to have them both."

"Sure I would. But I would never have more than one service dog. It wouldn't be fair, with so many other kids waiting for a partner.

"Brace," she commanded. This time Gabriel got to her first, steadying her with his shoulders as she climbed back into her wheelchair.

Then Noah tugged on the strap to the screen door and let the four of them inside.

A New Song

Case couldn't get Meg's words out of his mind: "so many other kids waiting for a partner." From the moment she said them, he knew he had to make a decision.

It nagged at him whenever he looked at Noah, which was almost every waking minute.

He thought about it when Harry came over to his house—when he showed Harry how Noah could pick out a root beer from all the other sodas in the fridge.

He thought about it when he bragged that Noah could pick up even a dime with his teeth.

Quinn had put a dime almost as shiny as the Woodsons' table on the kitchen floor. Case had said the right words: "Get it."

He thought about it when he showed his mother that Noah could make a bed. True, the corners of the sheets were still pouffy, but Noah did get the covers almost in place.

He thought about it when Noah won another blue ribbon in another agility trial. Nobody took their picture this time, and his name wasn't in the newspaper, but those things didn't seem to matter so much anymore.

He thought about it when he looked out at the silo near where Bitsy was buried and asked his mother how long and how badly it hurt to lose a dog. She answered him with a tight hug.

Quinn said he shouldn't worry so much, that his face might freeze into a frown if he didn't quit thinking about it all the time. His father said that since Noah was his dog, he had to figure out for himself the right thing to do.

Every now and then at the stables, Case even talked to Noah. "Say hello," he'd tell him, and wait for the dog to lay his head in Case's lap. He wished Noah could talk, could tell him what to do. That would make the decision easier, for sure. Noah could pick up a dime and maybe knock down a bowling pin, but he couldn't help Case make up his mind.

Nearly two weeks after the visit to the Woodsons', they were down at the stables late one Friday, Case and his father, grooming the last of the horses before supper. Noah brought Case a rubber curry comb in his teeth, and, taking it in his left hand, Case brushed small circles with it, stirring up puffs of dust from Sherlock's shoulders. When it was time to pick the dirt out of Sherlock's hooves, Case leaned his weight against his pony, trying to hold one hoof in his right hand and clean it with the hoof pick in his left one. It was hard for him to do—almost impossible. Even after seven weeks in a cast, his right arm hurt when he stretched it out like that.

Case wished he had never known what it was like to have an arm all banged up. He wished so much he had never known. But he did know.

And that made all the difference.

Nobody told Case to make the call, but he knew he had to. He asked his mother for the Woodsons' phone number.

"Be sure to tell Meg hello for all of us," Mrs. Callahan said.

Case heard the phone ringing and thought about hanging up. But he knew he couldn't.

"May I speak to Mr. Woodson?" Case asked. His voice was strong, and he tried to make it deep and calm, just like his father's.

"I've been thinking about Meg a lot lately," he said deliberately when Mr. Woodson picked up the phone. "About how much Gabriel means to her, about all the things she can do because she has him as her partner with paws."

"Gabriel and Meg make a great pair, that's for sure," Mr. Woodson said.

Case concentrated on his breathing. Slowly. In and out. In and out. That way he wouldn't have to think so much about his words. "And I've decided to give Noah to someone who needs him more than I do." He hoped his voice still sounded calm.

"That's a big decision, Case," Mr. Woodson said. "Are you certain?"

"Yes. I was wondering if you could help me find somebody like that. Since you paid a lot of money for Noah, that seems only fair. Maybe you could ask the people who trained Gabriel. They might know who would be the best match."

"Meg and I will find someone who needs him, if you're absolutely sure," Mr. Woodson said.

"I'm sure," said Case. The words sounded true this time. "Dad said he'll bring me to see Meg soon." Case was afraid the voice quivers might be coming, but they didn't. "Tell her I've figured out how we can train Gabriel to jump like Noah."

"You're welcome here anytime, Case," Mr. Woodson said.

When Case handed the phone to his father,

he could still hear Mr. Woodson's loud voice. "Your son is the bravest man I know," he said.

It was the loneliest day of Case's life, the day after Scarlett foaled, the day the trainer came for Noah. That afternoon a woman drove up in a dark green van. She said they'd find Noah just the right partner, that they had a waiting list of several hundred kids praying for a dog like Case's.

"You've answered somebody's prayers," she said. "Just keep thinking about that." She opened the back door to the van and waited for Case to say goodbye.

Noah was still wearing the collar that said *Noah Callahan* when he licked Case's face for the last time and backed into the crate.

"We'll invite Harry over to spend the night," Mrs. Callahan said just as the van pulled out of sight. Case knew that his mother had tears in her eyes—real ones, not the kind she pretended to cry in plays. She put her arm around his shoulders and they walked back to the porch.

"I've got a cake inside that needs frosting,"

Quinn said, rushing past them and slamming the door behind her. Case knew she was choking back tears, too.

"You seem so much taller these days, Case," his mother said as she stopped on the bottom step. She stooped over just a little to rest her chin on his head. "You're growing up so fast."

"He'll never stand taller than he does today," Mr. Callahan said. Case thought he sounded proud. A little sad, maybe, but definitely proud. "Never!"

Case fingered the blue ribbon in his shirt pocket, suddenly remembering that he had stuffed it there. "I forgot to give this to Noah."

"Noah doesn't need ribbons to know he's a champion. The wins that count the most don't come with ribbons anyway."

"How's Scarlett's colt doing?" Case knew that his father had stayed late at the stable last night to help with the foaling.

"Real well. Still a little wobbly on his legs, of course. Can you think of a name for him?"

"I was thinking Harry might be a good one."

"After your friend?"

"Well, no. After Harry Potter."

"Harry Potter he is!"

When Harry Algabright came over after supper, he and Case decided to spend the night at the stables in sleeping bags, keeping watch from the hayloft over Scarlett and her newborn colt.

"It's really dark out here at night," Harry said.

"You scared?" Case asked. He thought it was dark, too. He wished Noah were there to protect them, but he didn't say so. He heard something flapping nearby. He hoped Harry hadn't heard it. He hoped it wasn't a bat. Probably an owl, he thought. Just an old barn owl.

"Want me to teach you how to burp?" Harry asked.

The new colt had nestled beside his mother, and Case was starting to doze off. He heard Harry reach for a soda in the cooler beside them and twist off the top. He thought of Meg again.

One big burp, then two more that made lower sounds. That's what Case heard. He recognized the song. The first three notes of "Oh Where, Oh Where Has My Little Dog Gone?"

"I'm sorry, Case," Harry said, stopping abruptly. "I didn't mean to burp that song. It was the wrong thing to do today."

"It's okay," said Case. "I don't mind."

"I don't think I could have done what you did," Harry said. "You were really brave."

Case smiled. It wasn't so long ago, at the talent show, that he'd wished he could be as brave as Harry.

"Do you think you'll get another dog?" Harry asked after swigging more soda.

"Someday," Case answered. As much as not having Noah hurt right now, Case knew that the hurt wouldn't keep him from loving another dog. "Mom saw what good care I took of Noah. I'm pretty sure she won't stick to that no-dogs-allowed rule anymore." He paused. "Besides, she learned to love Noah as much as I did."

Harry handed Case a bottle of soda.

"I have a great idea," Case said after a while. He wanted to change the subject. "Next year for the talent show, I can teach you how to juggle baseballs, and we can both burp 'Take Me Out to the Ball Game.' Want to teach me now?"

So they lay there in the dark, the two of them, with an owl flapping overhead and a colt nickering quietly at the world that had just welcomed him.

They lay there laughing in the hayloft, trying hard to burp a new song.